RIDE OR DIE

(A 'Girl Obsessed' novella)

STORM

Copyright

Blurb

Out in the wilderness, we healed, we loved, we found our happiness.

But past connections suddenly threaten to uproot our peaceful existence.

The time to hide is over. Life propels us towards a series of revenge games and facing our demons head on.

It's unclear if we will survive the storm a second time around. But the one thing we do know for sure is that we're never giving up on each other.

It was ride or die then. It will be forever.

Warning: Trauma, murder, cnc and knife play, exhibitionism and two villainous leads who might just win you over.

***This novella is meant to be read after 'Girl Obsessed'*

To Veronica and Zoe for being Wynnie and Jude's biggest fans.

Wynter

1.

You'd think after spending ten months alone in the middle of nowhere with the same man, waking up to the same face every single morning and talking to nobody else but him would eventually bore you or at least irritate you a little, right? I had even anticipated it and warned him of my sour mood in advance. Asked him to forgive me if familiarity started to breed a tiny inkling of contempt because I may be a teenager but I wasn't naïve. These things happened in the most happiest of relationships and one just had to deal.

Well apparently, we had defied the odds yet again. There was no boredom. No irritation. Nothing that made me want to clobber him over the head with a sledgehammer. I still had hearts in my eyes, fire between my thighs and a breath-stealing obsession in my soul for this man.

He was looking particularly delicious this evening. Outside, the wind whipped against our cabin windows and doors, lending a thrill, a sense of danger to the atmosphere. We were two souls, all alone in the wilderness on a dark, stormy night.

There were no rules. No restrictions here.

From my position on the bed, I watched as he leaned back in his chair and locked his hands behind his head in that characteristic way of his. His t-shirt stretched tight over his chest and made my mouth water a bit. Since we had moved out here, Jude spent more time outdoors, free and at ease with his place in life. His muscles were more tightly corded now due to the physical labor he engaged in on the daily. It wasn't just a writer's body I looked at anymore.

His gaze slid towards me and he noticed me staring. He didn't smirk or anything upon catching the lust and adoration I never bothered to hide. No. That wasn't his style. Instead, he remained serious and assessing, like he was trying to figure out what I was in the mood for. Sex, obviously but...what kind of sex?

We'd explored pretty much everything by now...except for my ultimate fantasy. My heart was pounding so damn hard, I felt like it could rival the thunder outside. Could I do this? Could I really do this with him?

And more importantly, would he want to?

"Are you okay, baby? You look a little flushed," he finally spoke up, a slow burn igniting in his sharp, blue eyes because he knew exactly why I was all hot and bothered.

That whole nerdy, sexy vibe he had going...

Fuck.

I bit down on my lower lip a little and rubbed my legs together as I pondered on how to voice my darkest desires. He would never balk, no. But it was still kind of scary. Sometimes Jude could be scary. Especially when I got him to lose control.

"Remember how I once said I'd love for you to do things to me even when I told you no?" I questioned lightly, carefully watching for his reaction.

He was still, not revealing anything of his thoughts as he watched me back but there was that slight movement of his throat. A dead giveaway that I made him feel on edge even after all this time. It caused me to smirk at him in response.

"I think tonight's going to be that night, sweetie," I told him softly.

At times, Jude felt like a result of my corruption. And at other times, he was still the vulnerable writer I had first stumbled upon who wouldn't dare harm a living soul.

"Is that what you need tonight?" he asked me, his tone steady yet non-committal.

I reached down, down to the dark depths of my wanton soul, the parts which seemed to fascinate him and focused on nothing but him and what he represented for me. The things he made me feel, how my essence was stripped bare for this man to feast upon and he never turned away with disgust. You didn't find love like that unless you were one very lucky bitch.

"No," I made myself speak up as I backed up on the bed. "I don't need it. And especially not from you."

He narrowed his eyes at me, those sharp, angular features drawn tight and morphing into a harshness which his gentle nature wasn't actually capable of. But he would become that person. For me, he would turn himself into whatever I wanted him to be.

Pushing back his chair, Jude stood up and moved closer, determination in his every stride.

"I don't think you mean that, baby," he said to me unsmilingly and I watched as those strong, elegant fingers of his moved to the buttons of his shirt, opening them up one by one while he kept his sober gaze trained on me.

It wasn't a surprise that my body was responding to his attitude and movements like it wanted to be offered up as a sacrifice to the carnality I was about to witness in this man. I loved that Jude wore those button-downs even out here because I had told him I liked seeing him in it and undressing him slowly like I was unwrapping a naughty present.

"Of course I mean it," I made myself snap at him, getting into the role. "I don't want you to touch me all right. You're not allowed to."

He shrugged off his shirt and I instinctively swallowed as the tanned flesh of his upper body enticed me simply by its appearance. So ripped. Jude had always been lean and fit but the wilderness had made those muscles stand out even more.

My nipples had to peak as my senses reacted to his masculinity and an answering arousal simmered in his eyes. As usual, I was only wearing a thin t-shirt and I knew he could tell exactly how wet and tight I was in all the right places.

"Take your clothes off," he said to me and I inhaled a careful breath because this was so unlike him.

He didn't do this. He didn't take things I didn't want to give from me.

But you do want to give it, Wynnie, the voice in my head reminded me. *This is just role-playing.*

Then why was my heart thumping like crazy? Why was I not relaxing? Why was I suddenly a little unsure of my boyfriend when I was aware that he would never do a thing to hurt me?

"Jude-"

"Take your fucking clothes off and spread your legs for me," he commanded roughly this time before unbuttoning his jeans.

I knew what was in there. And just the anticipation of seeing that thing that I loved to worship with my mouth and my pussy and sometimes, my tits, made me let out a breathy moan.

His hands halted and he ran his tongue over his lips. Frowned at me thoughtfully and seemed to be wondering how best to move forth because I wasn't obeying his instructions.

"I won't," I threw back at him defiantly and scooted further upwards on the bed until my back touched the wooden headboard behind me. "You can't *make* me."

A sigh escaped him and despite the tense, uncertain atmosphere, I couldn't help but feel impressed. It was the long-suffering sigh of a villain. Like he knew that whatever was about to happen was inevitable and I was here needlessly wasting his time with my useless protests.

Jude finished unbuttoning his jeans and slid the zipper down but didn't remove it. I knew he wasn't wearing any underwear like me. We'd simply stopped bothering with such things a long time ago. Another rumble of thunder growled across the sky outside and I jumped at the noise while Jude prowled towards the bed, his silhouette in front of the fire dark and ominous, his face so grim.

"Wynnie, what I'm about to subject you to is going to be far more scary than the storm outside," he told me, his thighs finally hitting the edge of the mattress. "It's me you need to fear. Do as I'm asking and this will be over quickly."

Unexpectedly, my eyes welled up with tears upon hearing that last sentence. This was triggering me. This was reminding me of things I didn't want to remember. Things someone else had said to me not so long ago on a frightening and traumatic night in a place I had called home.

Almost immediately, Jude dropped his role and crawled onto the high bed, reaching for me without hesitation.

"Baby."

He wasn't a predator anymore. He wasn't just some guy wanting to fuck me and not care what it did to me. He was my Jude again.

"Wynnie, it's okay," he soothed me and I found myself being cradled in his arms. "It's me. I'm not going to hurt you. Please don't cry. I'm sorry I scared you-"

"No," I interjected sharply and pushed him away roughly which made him regard me with shock. "I'm *not* scared, okay. I can do this! I *need* this."

His brows came together in a deep frown. "We can try some other time-"

"It's happening tonight," I stated firmly, holding his gaze fiercely. "I'm *not* going to let memories of that fucker ruin *my* enjoyment of my fantasy. *Nothing* scares me, Jude. Nothing except the thought of losing you."

"Baby-"

"Don't argue with me," I interrupted in an impatient tone, breathing quickly. "You wanted me to be fearless...you said you loved that about me. Then help me overcome this. Help me win."

Jude's expression was tortured now as he debated the wisdom of going through with this despite how dangerous it could be for my mental and emotional health. What we were doing...it wasn't normal. Especially not for people who almost had to suffer through that in real life.

"Now is not the time to be a fucking pussy, Mr. Knight," I challenged. "Show me what you're really made of. Show me that savagery I know you're capable of." Lowering my tone, I drew closer and stared into his eyes scorchingly. "Force yourself on me. And don't stop no matter what. I trust you."

His hand clamped around my wrist and he squeezed slightly. I wasn't sure why but whenever he did that, it had a far greater effect on me than it would if a guy did that to other girls. I'd discovered that this was his go-to gesture whenever he made up his mind about something regarding me.

"Are you sure?" he asked me evenly, just once, and I nodded.

A long minute passed and I felt an adrenaline rush in my veins when I saw his eyes harden again. It was a cue for me and I made as if to move back but he didn't let go of my hand. I swallowed and struggled to free it, knowing he would bruise me there with that tight grip and my perverted, twisted side wanted to see that.

Jude submitting to me was always a delight and drove me freaking wild. Jude being forceful however was a whole other ecstasy altogether.

"Let me go," I said to him and tried to pull away again but he moved to straddle me firmly and pushed my body back on the bed, anchoring me to the mattress with his thighs while bringing his hands to my t-shirt and yanking it up without finesse.

"Tell me your trigger words," he ordered as the fabric left my body and I lay there naked and exposed.

I tried to get up but he grabbed my wrists once more and lifted my arms. A second later, I felt him tie the end of the rolled up t-shirt on one wrist, loop it through the wooden rails of the headboard and then fasten the other end to my other wrist.

"Triggers, Wynter," he snapped.

Fuck, his dominance was an extremely rare thing to witness but when it came to the surface, it had the power to melt any woman's panties. No wonder the ones in his life hadn't wanted to let him go. Jude Knight was the definition of complexity. A fascinating mix of submissive and aggressive.

"Don't say things like, 'Be quiet,'" I answered him in a low tone. "Don't shut me up when I'm trying to speak. And don't tell me it'll be over quickly."

Instead of acknowledging my words, Jude elicited a gasp from me when his calloused hands grabbed my breasts, kneading them and puckering my nipples even more with his fingers. I was keenly aware of another roll of thunder outside, the abrupt flickering of the flames in the fireplace and the woodsy, earthy scent that hung inside our cozy cabin.

A combination of safe and thrilling. That was what being with Jude was like.

Slowly, he leaned forward, bringing his lips close to my ear, the musky scent of pine and cologne drifting to my nostrils, his weight on me heavy, his crotch pressing lewdly against mine where his erection had popped out of its confines.

"Now tell me your safe word," he whispered in a voice that was devilishly dangerous, making it sound almost like a threat which ended up exciting me even more.

Let's see what you've got, baby.

"Wisconsin," I replied without a second thought.

My lover pressed his lips to my ear once, a sweet and comforting gesture, and then he straightened and caused me to suck in a stunned breath when his hands grasped my calves and pushed my legs back.

The game had started and it was time for me to get my head back in it. I didn't want to be Jude's victim. I wanted to fight him. He wasn't going to get what he desired from me. So I began to struggle and tried to pull my legs out of his grip but he held on so tight and kept them spread apart, his eyes burning as he focused on my exposed pussy which we both already knew was wet and ready for him to assault.

God...why was this so arousing? Why?

Was it some kind of primitive instinct born from eons ago when barbarians ruled the earth and took their women without permission? Ravished them and claimed them as if it was their due? I should hate this. But one look at Jude and I knew I'd let him do whatever he wanted to me.

"Look at you," he said softly, still not taking his hooded gaze off my pussy as he held tightly to my legs. "You tell me you don't want this and yet, your cunt is soaked, Wynter. Like it's weeping for my cock."

I bit back a moan and tried to close my legs. No luck. Jude was stronger than me now. Harder to dominate in bed. I savored the fights we had, that delicious push and pull.

"You should be ashamed of yourself, Mr. Knight," I scolded him angrily. "Lusting after a teenager like this."

His ghost of a smile was cool and unbothered. "How am I supposed to feel bad about that when the teenager in question can't stop flashing her tits at me every chance she gets?" he asked. "You think I haven't noticed? You think I'm not aware that you're always trying to tease me and acting like you're innocent. You're just as guilty because you want an older man's cock. This is proof of that, Wynnie."

He stretched me wide enough to hurt my thighs and latched his mouth onto my cunt like it was his last meal on earth. A sharp cry left my mouth at the sudden and intense pressure. He was not at all gentle with me. I'd told him once I wanted him to hurt me. Rip me apart. And I had a feeling I was about to experience exactly how depraved Jude Knight could get.

"Fuck, stop!" I yelled at him, hardening my heart and telling myself I didn't want this and feeling shocked when that refusal led my body to respond to him even more.

The fact that he didn't care about my protests, that he wanted me so bad he was willing to cross whatever lines necessary to satisfy his hunger was turning me on even as I struggled to free myself. I tried to drag myself back but he reached up and clamped a hand on my tummy, pressing down hard and locking his other arm under one of my knees. His teeth scraped against my sensitive flesh and I clenched my jaw.

"This is the tastiest cunt I have ever had the fortune to bury my face in," he growled from between my legs. "I can't wait to push my cock inside you, honey. Can't wait to feel you stretch and struggle to accommodate me. I won't stop until I'm balls deep in you. And you can't do a single thing about it."

My wrists were aching from the pressure of pulling against the bonds. I wished I could scratch him, slap his face, pull at his hair and the frustration and anger made me let out a snarl.

"You can't do this," I stated desperately. "Please! I...I...I have a boyfriend!"

He laughed, actually *laughed* at my statement and it sounded so villainous and mocking, I tried not to marvel at it.

"Even better," he replied and licked me in one long swipe of his tongue against my clit before stabbing it inside and fucking me with it.

"Jude!" I cried out instinctively, my eyes rolling back in pleasure and instantly, his fingers reached up to pinch my nipples again. Hard. "You son of a bitch!"

My resistance increased in strength so he pressed me down harder on the bed, the grip of his hands punishing and cruel.

You wanted to see my depravity, he seemed to be saying with his body. *Then so be it.*

The darkness in Jude was a black flame born out of an innate restlessness which he stamped down almost every day. It wasn't like mine, allowed to roam freely and unapologetically. He controlled his. He needed to because unleashing it made him hate himself, doubt himself. Like he still needed to prove he wasn't a bad person.

Apart from his stories, I was the only catalyst he could find to channel that vibrant, fierce energy.

"Untie me, you sick fuck," I cursed at him, making my voice rigid. "I thought you were a good man, Mr. Knight. But you're just as greedy as the rest. Salivating over a pussy that's way out of your league."

That got to him. Me humiliating him got to him so bad because I was forcing him to face his demons here just like he was forcing me to face mine.

The look on his face as he raised himself on his knees and glared at me managed to instill further traces of doubt in me. No. No, I trusted this man. He was Jude. He wasn't *actually* going to hurt me.

"Safe word," was all he said as a reminder before he stabbed his fingers inside my pussy and made me cry out, my eyes filling with tears because he was so rough and crude.

It was three fingers at first and I gasped when he inserted a fourth one. I panicked for a minute wondering if he was going to go a step further and fist me or something but all he did was reach out and curl the fingers of his other hand around my throat, pressing slightly while he continued to finger me down there.

"So juicy," he commented and then carried those fingers to his mouth and sucked on them.

The battle going on inside my chest between my heart and my ribcage was a new thing for me. I'd never been this excited about anything in my life. How unpredictable he was. How immoral. How...like me.

"I don't hear you saying no to me anymore," he spoke up after several seconds. "What's the matter? Decided you would love some dick after all?"

I actually *would* love some. Some of what he had going for him down there. It was bulging and ready and my traitorous cunt was here for it.

"Don't you dare put that thing in me, you fucking pervert!" I cried and kicked out at him.

Jude winced, released my throat and caught my ankles before shooting me another glare.

"I'm going to be right back," he told me and I watched in anticipation as he got out of bed and stalked over to the cupboard in the far corner of the cabin.

My eyes grew wide when he extracted a coil of rope from it and then went to the kitchen at the back to retrieve a knife. Again, it felt like my heart was going to leap out of my throat because he looked so damned determined and dangerous.

I swallowed as the knife blade glinted while he cut the rope and used the pieces to tie my ankles to each corner of the foot of the bed. I might even have let out a whimper and he probably caught it because he looked up from his task and frowned at me.

The knife was a trigger as well but I didn't tell him so, willing him not to break the role. We were too far into this thing now and I wanted to see how it played out. I didn't need him to be a concerned boyfriend right now.

"My god, Jude. Have you learned nothing from me?" I taunted boldly as he stood there holding the knife in his hand, his task of securely tying me up now complete. "Do you remember the number of times I made you sleep with me when you kept saying no? I got you drunk and seduced you. I even touched you in your sleep once. I took whatever I wanted from you. And you can't even bring yourself to exact revenge once? God, you're such a wimp."

My words had the desired effect on him and he angrily shoved down his pants, moving to place the knife away.

"No." I stopped him with fire in my eyes and shook my head. "Bring the knife with you."

Jude appeared stressed. I knew he was remembering everything I had told him about my night was Joshua. He was aware this might be triggering for me. Who knew? I might even snap and plunge that blade in him in the heat of anger because I had never really dealt with my trauma. Never seen a therapist. Never confronted my problems. I'd only run away and taken shelter in this man's love. But inside, I was the same fucked up Wynter Cassidy.

He climbed back on the bed without a word and when he reached the apex of my thighs, he gave me one last questioning look.

I lifted my chin determinedly. "Put it here."

My lover's eyes weren't quite focused, as though this tortured him as much as it did me. If he backed out, I was never going to forgive him. I wasn't this weak bitch. I *wasn't*. It has been over a year since that night when my entire life changed. I wasn't going to run away from it anymore.

"Do it you pussy," I snapped at him. "You know there's no other way I'm letting you take me unless you hold that knife to my throat."

"Stop calling me a pussy," he snapped back and my breath caught in my throat when he placed the sharp, shiny blade against my neck.

I went completely still. I fucking froze. Flashes of Joshua Andrews making me feel helpless and thinking he could treat me like some cheap whore slammed into me and I gritted my teeth, trying to keep my breathing as normal as possible.

"That the best you got?" I made myself whisper and his expression went wild.

Seconds later, I felt the head of his cock nudging at my entrance but I was so tense, he couldn't plunge through like he usually did. Tense because the situation had taken some of my arousal out of the equation. All I could feel was the knife at my throat and the fact that I was now completely helpless.

"Use your safe word, Wynter," Jude reminded me yet again, still not entering me.

I closed my eyes briefly and wanted to say it. I really wanted to. I wanted him to stop. And yet, that sick, stubborn part of me which loved to push limits kept me from admitting defeat.

"There's no way your little cock is going to be enough to make me feel good," I said to him and smirked, crushing down my fear.

Jude was the one who closed his eyes this time before he whispered, "God help me." And then he pushed inside me. My eyes teared up at the discomfort but I took it without a word. I saw only two outcomes out of this. Either I would realize just how brave I could be or how broken I still was. I needed to know.

"That feels good," he breathed in pleasure and looked down at me with lust-filled eyes. "Doesn't that feel good, baby? Better than your boyfriend's." His chest was slick with sweat now and he grunted once, probably drowning in the sensations but he kept the knife steady.

I felt him swell inside me even more and knew he was enjoying this far more than he wanted to. That loosened up some of the tension in me. Watching him experience the dark pleasure I told him he wasn't allowed to experience. The forbidden, illicit thrill of it. I knew in that ever-energized mind of his, he really was imagining me belonging to someone else and being forced to take him.

His breaths turned into gasps, his movements quickened. For a moment, I thought he might cut me but Jude finally placed the knife aside and gripped my throat with his bare hand once more, choking me a little. Inwardly, I felt relief flood through me but that quickly turned to apprehension when he began to stab his dick in me like he wouldn't have stopped even if the apocalypse had come upon us.

"Tell me this is better than what you're used to. Tell me this feels amazing. Admit it," he rasped as his hips pistoned against mine and I moaned loudly, hating that I couldn't touch him.

God, he was hurting me. His hand was squeezing a little too tight and his thrusts were brutal. I tried to back up again but he gripped my hips to hold me in place and fucked me harder.

"Fucking hell, Wynnie," he said throatily, the twisted version of him revealing itself so beautifully, I almost laughed with delight if I hadn't been in pain.

He didn't even care what I was feeling anymore. He just took from me.

"Stop," I said to him one last time and pulled at my bindings. "I don't want this."

"Oh yeah?" he retorted breathlessly. "Then why the fuck are you getting so wet? Feel that? Feel how easily my cock is going in now? That's because you do want this, baby."

He wasn't wrong. I really was getting slicker and I couldn't understand this perversion.

"Please let me go, Jude. Please," I made myself beg, writhing and twisting my body in a way that indicated I wasn't responsive to his fucking.

"Fuck, just a few more seconds, honey," he gritted as his face tightened. "I have to cum inside you. You know I have to, Wyn. You're fucking driving me nuts. *Hold the fuck still*," he growled at me angrily as I struggled and he reached up to squeeze my breasts together roughly with his hand.

I hissed in pain and he laughed again because the breast-squeezing started to make me come really hard.

"No," I whined. "No, no, I can't enjoy this...stop doing this to me. Stop, you asshole."

He grunted at my words and then let out a loud, satisfied groan, stilling all of a sudden while I felt the gush of his semen inside me. That sticky wetness that pooled between my legs made me whine with extreme pleasure.

"You're such a filthy animal, Mr. Knight," I told him in a voice weakened by exertion.

He pulled out of me slowly and then began to untie my bonds, absently rubbing my wrists and ankles as he did so, the frown on his face now worried.

"Please," he said grimly and then lay down beside me, breathing heavily and wiping the sweat from his face. "Don't ever make me do that again."

"Why? Afraid you like it too much?" I teased, turning to study his tense profile.

"Wynter, you were scared," he replied, staring blankly at the ceiling. "I saw it. I saw the fear in your eyes. Why didn't you use your safe word? You know what happens when you push me, right? Why did you keep pushing me?" he wanted to know.

Letting out a sigh, I shifted so that my head was on his chest and I could play with the smattering of hair on it. The guy's heart was thundering inside and I smiled upon discovering that.

"That actually wasn't so bad," I murmured even though my vagina was throbbing like hell. "Jude. I don't think you've ever pounded me so hard since we got together."

His fingers went into my hair and massaged my scalp, the gesture both comforting and indulging. Man, I loved him so much.

"Thank you for not treating me like I'm weak. For not backing out. This felt like the ultimate test of trust between us and I'm glad we passed," I told him as the night outside grew calmer, along with my heartbeats.

"I love you, Wyn," he told me in a husky voice.

I smiled and murmured the words back because I never got tired of saying it. My eyelids grew heavy as I watched the flickering flames and I was almost asleep when his next words made me jerk my head back to stare at him.

"I want to kill him."

Uncertain and a little freaked out by his vehemently uttered sentence, I pushed back my hair and raised my eyebrows in question.

Jude was the least violent person I knew so hearing him say something like this was incredibly disturbing.

"Um...who-?"

"Joshua Andrews," he said, his gaze fixed on the knife he had discarded earlier. "When you told me about it in that church, it hurt. But when I got to experience how he made you feel, when I watched you trying to recreate your nightmare and not let it destroy you this time, that shit made me want to find him and slit his fucking throat with that same knife he held to you."

I snorted a little and moved away from him because I needed to pee.

"You sound like Liam Neeson in that movie. *I will find you and I will kill you.*"

"I'm not kidding, Wynter."

His voice was stiff and resolute and I paused to study him again, lying there naked and angry, sounding so vicious. What was wrong with him? This wasn't like him.

"Jude, come on. It's in the past now," I placated and jumped out of bed. "We left that life behind remember? We're happy here."

I was almost at the door of the bathroom when he spoke again and made me pause a second time, sending a hint of uneasiness through me.

"Don't you think it's fucking unfair that they all got away with what they did to us and we have to pretend that shit didn't mess with our mental and emotional health at all?"

He sounded so bitter all of a sudden. So harsh. Shit. I had been afraid that the rape play thing was going to be triggering for me but it seemed to have sent him in one of his dark moods instead. He had that 'everyone's out to get me and wants to wrong me' look on his handsome face and it made me sad.

"Baby," I said softly, making him look at me. I gave him a sweet smile. "We can't win all the time. We can't fight them all. As long as we have each other though, the days will be good and the nights on fire. Let it go."

He didn't respond so I ducked in the bathroom, experiencing a weird feeling in my chest. We'd had months and months of peace and I had to go and screw it all up because *I* was so screwed up inside thanks to my past. I hadn't let it go but I had to say those words for him. The last thing I wanted was for Jude to lose the peace he had finally found and begin to spiral again.

Jude

2.

The wood pile was receiving the brunt of my anger and frustration the next morning. In the small clearing behind our cabin, I grunted and struck logs with my hatchet and imagined it to be Joshua Andrews' skull.

God, what was happening to me? Last night, the bondage, the dark, shameful desires we indulged in, the demons that came to the surface, it wasn't supposed to rattle me so bad. It was just bedroom play, right? She was always good at her roles whenever we fucked. I was the one who had a hard time detaching.

But that fear in her grey eyes....

That hadn't been fake.

Wynnie was still bearing the scars of her past and I'd reopened those wounds for a few minutes. But they had been enough to make me realize that she wasn't completely fine.

And neither was I.

Hell, I wanted to kill the man. I really wanted to kill him. I *should* have done it a long time ago instead of acting like a...

What had she called me?

A fucking pussy.

That wasn't a total lie. I'd always been a pussy when it came to confrontation. She was the only one who managed to get me to step out of my comfort zone but even that didn't last too long. Did she really feel that way about me deep down?

That I wasn't alpha enough? Not man enough to do what needed to be done? Instead I had spoken of law and justice. What would other protective lovers do? They'd find those motherfuckers who hurt their girl so much and then beat them up. Make them regret ever laying their filthy hands where they didn't belong.

What had I done? Worried about myself. My image. My fucking career and public relations. The legal system. Then I'd wanted to kill myself and had needed her to save me so I could come and hide out here.

I hacked harder at the wood as the doubts crept in. Yeah, we were happy. And not just happy. Blissful. This place, the serenity and naturalness had been like a healing balm for both our tortured souls, especially mine. There was always something new to do, some new place to explore. We took strolls together and hiked and fucked against trees or in valleys in complete and utter abandonment. We camped out on the days it wasn't cold. We took baths in the river up ahead where Wynnie was at this very moment, fishing.

Yup, she'd taught herself how to fish and hunt and we had that vegetable garden going for me too. She was always finding stuff to fix around the cabin or remodeling it when she wasn't spending her time being the sexiest little vixen that ever existed.

We took turns cooking for each other and laughed when it didn't turn out good because trying out new recipes was our thing. We also had this huge tub embedded in a raised wooden platform in our bathroom where we spent many evenings, fucking or reading or just soaking during lazy conversations. There were always enough supplies thanks to Brent and once, Wynnie and I had snuck out to the closest town as well to stock up on groceries, feeling all infamous and smug the whole time because we got away with it.

The perfect outlaw couple. We had the best life two lovers could ever dream of and I knew that. But the damage that had been inflicted on her and on me, the way we hadn't truly dealt with any of it because neither of us had been strong enough...that plagued me now.

This wasn't okay. Sure I still made money and sold books. My current fans loved my notoriety and I found myself enjoying every admirable sentiment they expressed.

But deep down, I felt like a fraud. True notoriety didn't come with hiding away and acting like a wimp. It had been months. I wasn't in the same place I had been back when everything had fallen apart and I had felt depressed and suicidal.

I was stronger now. Not the guy who winced like a child just because his knuckles couldn't handle a punch. I could rip people apart if I had to. Maybe I should start with that fucktard who made my girl feel like she had to give up on life, who drove her out of her own home and tried to take so much from her.

My hacking grew frantic, louder.

Wynter was going to be back soon. I should probably go inside and make a fire. I loved taking care of her. She was fierce as fuck but needy as well and being needed by her meant everything to me.

I didn't give myself time to think or hesitate when branches crunched under someone's foot behind me. Wynnie was at the river in front of me and Brent would never come unannounced given how cautiously we lived out here. He would never approach without a word either.

The hatchet went flying completely on instinct and the intruder let out a terrified shriek as she put up her hands in defence and cowered.

I froze slightly as the axe found its mark and buried itself in the tree trunk beside Ella.

Ella.

Oh my God.

I breathed raggedly as I watched the woman I had called my best friend for so many years of my adult life lower her arms slowly and pin me with a stunned look. Her face was so pale and her eyes swiveled from me to the hatchet only inches from her shoulder. She gulped and opened her mouth in shock when she met my eyes again.

I didn't know what to say. It had been over a year since I had seen her last. Not since the day I had found out she had been the one who had publicly put me in a position which was guaranteed to lead to my downfall. The one person I had never expected to betray me.

"Jude," she said softly and sadly, appearing thin and fragile in her t-shirt and jeans.

She didn't look too good and for a split second, I felt a little concerned for her until I remembered what she had done and the fact that she had somehow found me. She'd discovered our hideout. Fuck.

"What the hell are you doing here?" I asked her abruptly, stalking over to her and wrapping my hands around the handle of the hatchet before yanking it out.

Ella flinched and stepped away from me warily as she eyed the tool and then my chest before staring up at my face.

"Jude, please don't be mad at me," she croaked out, wringing her hands together as her eyes filled up with tears. "How have you been? God, I missed you. You have no idea just how much. I spent months trying to look for you-"

"Why?" I narrowed my eyes at her. "So you can go tell the whole world where J. R. Knight is hiding so they can all come at me again? Why the fuck did you come here, Ella? And more importantly, who else have you told?"

She shook her head at me and stepped closer, wiping at her tears. "Nobody! I promise. Jude, I'm sorry. I'm so sorry about what I did to you, okay," she cried softly. "I felt horrible. I hated myself for it. You chose her...a stalker and a criminal over me...your best friend who was trying to protect you. I felt betrayed and jealous. Angry. So I...I screwed up okay. I thought it would make you leave her. I never knew you loved her so much." Her voice broke down when she said that last sentence.

"Ella, you shouldn't have come here," I growled at her. "Also, I don't for a second trust you and fuck it, I built a life here for myself. Now I have to uproot everything because of you."

She lifted her hands and made as if to touch me but I backed off quickly. Ella's expression was tortured.

"You don't have to," she told me miserably. "I promise I will never tell. I just wanted to see you. Missed you like hell all these months, Jude. Don't I get a hug for old time's sake?"

If Ella laid even one finger on me, I didn't know what my girlfriend was going to do to her when she had been the only one touching me for so long and had repeatedly told me she was very possessive of me. Also, she'd promised me months ago that she wouldn't hesitate to kill anyone who dared to intrude upon us. I had to get Ella out of here.

"God, look at what she's done to you!" Ella suddenly burst out, her eyes running all over my bare chest and then going to my overgrown stubble. "You look like...like-"

"A savage?" I filled in for her and pinned her with a grim look. "She didn't do shit to me, Ella. This is what happens when a man is driven to the brink of death, learns to find his way back and decides to show his middle finger to the whole world. The world you turned against me," I reminded her but it was like she was mesmerized by the sight of my chest.

She even licked her lips once, her gaze growing uncertain and I frowned at that and shook my head a little. What was it with these women and me? There were so many other guys in the world.

"I missed you so much," she repeated as the wind whistled around us and a few stray squirrels squeaked nearby accompanied by the calling of birds. It was summer time now and the outdoors were a great place to be but I was already in a hell of a mood since last night and her appearance had made it worse.

"You need to get out of here right now," I stated but it was too late.

I opened my mouth once more to cry out a warning but Wynter had slammed a piece of wood against Ella's head and the woman crumbled to a heap on to the forest floor right in front of me.

"Jesus, Wynnie," I cursed and bent at once to check Ella's pulse, feeling a rush of protectiveness within me which I quickly squashed. "What the hell? You could've killed her!"

Wynnie was silent as I finished making sure Ella wasn't dead and rose to my feet once more, regarding her angrily. My now nineteen year old lover looked back at me calmly as the wood she had struck Ella with hung from her hand. Her light blond hair was damp from her bath and all she wore was a tiny, blue summer dress with a deep neckline. Her feet were bare and her toes had pale pink nail polish on them.

Still so innocent-looking. So curvy and toned at the same time and so damn young and alluringly sexy.

"Bitch had it coming," she told me coolly and then glanced at my crotch before narrowing her eyes. "Tell me that's happening because of my presence, Mr. Knight, and not because your little friend here showed up."

I puffed out a breath and bent once more so I could pick Ella up to take her inside and try to revive her but Wynter was way ahead of me as she threw the log aside and gripped Ella's limp form by the arms.

"Don't you dare," she warned me, her grey eyes cold. "I don't want any part of her on you. At all. I won't spare her next time."

I shook my head at her dramatics and waited for her to grip Ella properly before following her back to the cabin, my mind already trying to come up with everything we needed to do in order to clear out this place.

My heart grew heavy as I thought about it. This wild spot had been home for us but someone had found their way here and now we weren't safe anymore. My Wynnie wasn't safe anymore. We had to leave as soon as possible.

"She's not waking up, Wyn," I muttered, sitting back on my heels near Ella's immobile body with some smelling salts in my hand.

Wynter didn't say anything but when I glanced up I caught the smirk she was trying to hide while retrieving a coil of rope from the cupboard.

"This isn't funny, you know," I said with a scowl.

My girlfriend just dragged over a chair and gestured for me to let her put Ella in it. I pinned her with a disbelieving look. She waited patiently but when I refused to comply, she went over to the kitchen and grabbed the knife we had used last night.

"Okay, whoa. What do you think you're doing?" I held up a hand to keep her away from Ella and she narrowed her eyes at me.

"Jude, let me tie her to this chair or god help me, I am going to hurt this woman," she promised in a deadly tone. "We can't risk her being able to escape from here before we do so please."

I studied her for a while, considering her words and then sighed and let her do as she wanted. She wasn't entirely wrong. We were at risk of being discovered now and we couldn't take any chances. Ella would remain bound and immobile for as long as it took for us to gather all essential stuff and get the fuck out of this area.

"I can't believe this is happening," I murmured sadly and looked around the cabin in frustration. "Fuck, Wynter. I don't want to leave this place. We made some good memories here. I'm so sorry I couldn't-"

"It isn't your fault," she said to me and came closer to give me a hug from behind. "Baby, we'll figure it out. We've dealt with worse."

I put my hands over hers on my chest and felt her run her tongue over my sweaty skin, her generous breasts pressed against my back muscles. Blood rushed to my groin immediately and my jeans grew tight around my crotch but I closed my eyes and told myself to resist. There were more important things to take care of now. Safety first and all.

"Jude." Ella chose that exact moment to stir and slowly, her eyes flickered open. I turned to her carefully while Wynter released me and jumped on top of the counter beside me along one wall like she was preparing for a show.

What was going on in her mind? She hadn't said much to me about Ella's appearance since we'd come inside the cabin and it was making me suspicious. I had expected her to go batshit crazy and scratch the woman's eyes out but instead, she was acting all cool and casual which made me a thousand times more apprehensive.

"What did you do to me?" was the first thing Ella said to Wynter and I braced myself for some serious tension about to erupt. Ella demanding answers from Wynnie was not going to turn out well.

The sound of metal sliding against the tiled counter sent my heartbeats running wild. God help me but the more I witnessed Wynter's brand of crazy, the more it turned me on.

Ella's eyes were huge pools of green, terrified and panicked while it flickered from the knife to Wynter's unforgiving expression. I would've laughed if I didn't still feel some sort of fondness for the woman who was my former best friend. Wynnie's bark was worse than her bite.

"Weren't you the reason my lover had to suffer months and months of humiliation and agony which almost led to his untimely death?" Wynter asked her in a deadly soft voice and Ella swallowed.

"Wynnie. Baby, you don't need to do this," I told her. "Let's just go."

My girlfriend slid me a cool glance. "I need her to pay for her crimes," she informed me quietly but with determination. "What did you tell me once? Snap the fuck out of the fantasy?" She smirked. "Well, Ella here needs a dose of reality. Nobody messes with my Jude and gets away with it."

Sometimes I couldn't tell whether she was joking or serious. And whether I was a complete sicko for finding these traits of hers appealing.

"Wynnie, we're not killing her," I whispered fiercely and Ella let out a tiny whimper when she heard my words.

Wynter pouted slightly before reaching out to pull me closer. "Of course not, baby." Her tongue curled along my earlobe and I shuddered a little before freezing when she added, "We're just going to make her watch."

What in the world?

"We should be focusing on getting the hell out of here," I snapped in response and stepped away but she jumped off the counter and walked over to Ella who still looked terrified, twisting the chair so that it faced the large open doorway of the bathroom, directly in line with our huge tub.

"Wyn-"

"You're dirty," she whispered to me with a naughty smile and came over to take a hold of my wrist. "She's not going anywhere, baby. Come on. Let's get you all cleaned up."

I cast an uncertain look at Ella as she remained still in the chair but Wynter was already leading me towards the bathroom.

"You used to hate going out without having showered first and looking your best," my girlfriend reminded me innocently. "Even in this wilderness, you're always dressed well so why should today be any different?"

When we reached the area beside the tub, she brought her hands to my zipper and murmured, "Besides, I want to show her what she lost, Jude. What she will never get to put her hands on. Weren't you just talking about payback last night?" The sound of the zipper being dragged down seemed loud in the cabin and my heart raced at that. "What better way to get back at her than to make her crave you and deny her the satisfaction of having you? I know I'd be up for it."

Again, I glanced over at Ella who was staring at us with her mouth half open, her expression a mixture of disgust and fascination. She appeared torn between wanting to look away and not being able to. Ella had been my friend and I had never felt remotely attracted to her in all the years I had known her. Our relationship was purely platonic. She'd always cared about me and I for her so this was...kind of sick.

And yet, when Wynter knelt before me and her tongue peaked out to lick my cock, the erection that resulted was inevitable.

"It makes me so ravenous," she said thickly and palmed my dick almost reverently. "He tastes so damn good. Too bad you'll never know."

I didn't think my heart had jumped this erratically in all my life when I heard her words, felt her mouth against me and then noticed the way Ella gazed at me almost longingly before casting a look of hatred towards Wynnie.

That hateful look made me tense up. This girl had loved me through everything, witnessed my weakest moments and my darkest desires and never backed down. She was perfect in every way and didn't deserve the hate. Not after the way life had fucked things over for her. All she had was me and she needed this right now.

So did I. As Wynnie licked my cock and made appreciative noises before taking half my length inside her warm, wet mouth, I experienced an evil sort of satisfaction in the way Ella squirmed in her chair, her gaze fixed on the action happening down there. The woman had betrayed me in such a way that I had spiraled completely because of her thoughtless and selfish decision. She had cost me almost everything. And instead of being mad at her, I was still feeling bad for her, still acting concerned that she might get hurt here.

Why the fuck should I care? Where had it gotten me except to let women like her take advantage of my weaknesses and exploit them for their needs? At least Wynnie had made the ultimate sacrifice. The girl who was obsessed with me above all others had decided to let me go in the end for my sake. Because she had wanted me to find peace in the life she believed I needed. What the fuck had Ella done for me? If I ever hurt my girl, Wynter was never ever going to do anything to destroy me.

No matter how lethal she claimed to be, I knew in my heart of hearts that my lover would rather kill herself than watch me suffer.

"Suck me harder."

Wynnie stilled at my words and glanced up at me in surprise, letting my dick go for a moment. Gently, I gathered her blonde tresses away from her face and smiled down at her grimly.

"Do it," I whispered to her. "I need it."

With a wicked grin, she lifted her chin at me and defiantly said, "Make me."

I dragged in my breath through my teeth slowly and painfully because this was both sexy and torturous. Then my fingers in her hair grasped and held tight while I used my other hand to direct my cock towards her face. She pressed her lips together so I smeared my precum along them, pushing slightly.

"You love filling your dick inside this teenager's tight little mouth, don't you?" she teased me and I exhaled roughly and stuffed my dick inside in one swift, abrupt movement.

It felt dirty and I liked it. I liked her innocent-looking face and her youthfulness. I liked that she was crazy about me and my cock.

"Suck," I told her firmly and this time, Wynnie complied. Boy, did she know how to please me.

Months had gone by and I still wasn't quite used to her sinful enthusiasm and eagerness for having my dick in her hands, her mouth, her pussy or her ass, between her tits. She liked me to use her this way and in return, she used me to her heart's content as well.

I groaned deeply as her tongue slid up and down my length and the suction of her mouth increased. She suddenly let me go again and glanced at me only to say, "Dirty old man," before latching on to my dick again.

At thirty-two, I was hardly old but she liked reminding me of how much older than her I was as though she got off on it or something.

In the heat of the moment, I'd almost forgotten Ella but Wynnie hadn't because I caught her eyeing my former friend as she continued to blow me.

"Filthy girl," I whispered to her and she let out a moan and bobbed her head quicker, drooling all over my dick.

No matter what, no matter how many dirty deeds we did together, the tenderness and love I felt for her always overwhelmed me.

"Come up here and kiss me," I said urgently and she slowly released me again and got to her feet.

I clamped my hand behind her head and gave her a hard, possessive kiss, hugging her so tightly. My cock throbbed and strained between us and Wynnie rubbed against it, slowly starting to lift her dress. She wasn't wearing panties and I fingered her with my other hand, slipping them in and out of her wet hole.

Wynter finally pulled her mouth away, breathless and aroused and pushed me until I was pressed to the wall, sweeping her hands over my chest.

"Show her how you fuck me," she demanded, her grey eyes stormy and mad with desire for me. "Don't hold back. Show her how completely you belong to me."

I twisted us around until she was the one against the wall this time, hoisted her up so that her legs were wrapped around me and lined my cock up with her entrance. She was still as curvy as ever but I was no longer the weak as man who couldn't handle a fight and it showed in the way I fucked her against that wall, eliciting loud, lustful cries from her pretty mouth while Ella watched us.

I began to like it. I began to like it a lot actually. Our blatant exhibitionism, the sweet taste of revenge executed in this shameless, decadent manner. Ella's betrayal might have led to my ruin but she hadn't been able to tear me and Wynter apart. Never was I going to leave Wynter Cassidy over anything or anyone. Never was I going to let a single thing break us apart now.

It was ride or die then and it always will be.

Slamming into her like the savage I was, I bit down on her neck and laughed a little at the way she dug her nails into my skin and pulled at my hair. We were animals in the making and damn proud of it. I wanted to show everyone what we were together. Hiding out had been healing for both of us after everything we had faced but it was time to kiss the sunlight now.

It was time we returned to reality.

"I'm cumming, baby. Oh my God, it's...it's...oh *fuck* Jude!" Wynter moaned deeply and I felt her squirting upon my cock, one of those particularity intense orgasms that completely unravelled her.

A couple of seconds later, it was my turn and I let go just as fiercely and ecstatically, bruising her hips with my fingers just the way she liked it. The way my cum shot into her was the most raw and satisfying feeling in the whole goddamn universe.

We gasped into each other's necks when we were done and I knew Wynnie was looking at Ella as she asked in a mocking tone, "Enjoying the show?"

Quiet fell in the cabin as soon as our frantic fucking ceased and I felt my face burn, not just from the exertion but from what I had let my old friend see while getting carried away on a tide of lust and lewdness. I felt shame because of how much I had enjoyed putting up a performance and Wynter probably knew because she could read me like a book. She could always tap into the parts of me I pushed down, bring them to the surface and help me embrace them.

"Bath time for you, love," she whispered in my ear and kissed it as I lowered her to the floor.

I didn't look at Ella as I went over to the tub and filled it up with warm water before stepping of my jeans.

"Mmm. Well, isn't that a sight for sore eyes. A bitch can be lucky," my lover teased me like the little brat she was and when I glanced over at her, she was smirking at Ella again before she kicked the door shut and locked us inside.

"Oh so now you want some privacy?" I taunted while slowly sinking into the water and letting out a pleasurable groan as it soothed my very bones.

"I needed to make sure you're okay after that," she uttered softly and our eyes met and held, so many emotions passing through us that it was impossible not to reach out and pull her in the tub with me.

Wynnie let out a shriek and splashed water around the place and I laughed before tightening my arms around her to give her a passionate, no-holds-barred kiss.

"Mmm. I'm getting horny again." She squirmed against me and my recently sated dick responded slowly but surely.

Five minutes later, we were fucking again. It was wet, loud and messy. Everything else was forgotten for those few minutes. Ella, the changes we were going to have to make to our lifestyle, the shadows of our past.

"Where have you been all my life?" I questioned in awe, a little out of breath from the thorough riding she had given me.

Wynnie giggled and stuck her tongue out at me. "Busy growing up," she quipped and yelped when I pinched her nipples.

"I feel like having some wine," I told her.

I hadn't had any in ages. I knew what that stuff did to me and out here, we needed to be on our guard at all times. The fear that I might get drunk and pass out some night while Wynter was in danger kept me away from all things alcohol. She cupped my cheek and gave me a concerned look.

"It'll be okay," she reassured me, caressing my mouth with her thumb. "We'll find another safe haven, baby."

I nodded and braced myself against the onslaught of anxiety I knew was going to come because of this abrupt disruption to my peaceful life but...it didn't happen. I felt...oddly light and resolved to make sure that we really did survive this next obstacle in our journey. Whoa. This was new. All this time I had thought no amount of preparation would be enough to equip me for facing such a situation head on but I guess I'd been wrong.

Wynter planted a loud smack of a kiss on my cheek and then scrambled out of the tub to grab a towel.

"I'm going to go see if little Ella there stayed put or not. If she somehow managed to escape-"

"Wyn," I interrupted in a warning tone and she made a face at me.

"I'm not going to kill her, Jude," she scoffed but as she left the bathroom, she muttered, "Not if she keeps that mouth of hers shut."

Leisurely, I splashed some water over myself and scrubbed away the grime and sweat. After about five minutes, I emerged from the bathroom and found the cabin to be empty except for Ella tied up in her chair.

"Where's Wynnie?" I questioned as I rifled through my clothes and found a t-shirt and jeans.

She should have been packing our stuff and preparing to leave. I only hesitated for a second before dropping the towel and changing in front of Ella. Nothing she hadn't seen already.

"She went outside," Ella answered in a subdued tone and I turned to find her regarding me unhappily. Defeat was written all over her face. Defeat and heartbreak.

I wanted to feel sorry for her but I stopped myself yet again. I had never led her on or given her any indication that there could ever be more than friendship between us. I had no reason to feel guilty. We were even now.

Walking over to the cabin door, I peeked outside, only to be greeted with mountain air and the sounds of nature. It was almost midday and my stomach grumbled all of a sudden. It would have to be something quick and simple. Canned soup, maybe. We had a lot to get done.

"You hungry?" I asked our captive as I made my way over to the kitchen and opened the cupboards. "Might as well eat something while you're here."

"Jude," Ella said shakily from behind me and I glanced at her over my shoulder, wishing she wouldn't try to persuade me into letting her go. We both knew it was foolish.

"Wynter seemed upset," she informed me hesitantly, like it pained her to say it. "She was scrolling through her phone and I don't know what she saw on it but she...she looked like she was about to cry and rushed out-"

I was stalking towards the door before she had finished speaking, worry engulfing me all of a sudden. Why would she go outside? Why not come to me?

"Wynnie?" I called out and received no answer. Dread filled me at that silence and I rounded the cabin quickly, my gaze searching for her. "Wyn-"

She was on her knees on the ground near the spot where I had been chopping wood earlier, her face buried in her hands and her sobs muffled. They tore at me, making me clench my jaw as I wondered what could have upset her so much that she wanted to escape me even. When she cried, it sounded like she was carrying the weight of the world on her shoulders. At her age, I knew it couldn't be easy dealing with pain. Hell, it wasn't easy at my age either.

"Baby?" I murmured soothingly and knelt beside her, looking at her down-bent head, her damp hair covering the sides of her face. "Babe, what happened? What was on your phone? Talk to me."

She gasped slightly and still wouldn't look at me so I reached for her mobile which was discarded nearby and opened up to whatever screen she had been on last. We had WIFI here so going online wasn't difficult at all even if we had to keep covering our tracks by employing hackers. She'd been on Facebook, checking her mother's profile again and my heart twinged with pain because I knew no matter how much time passed or whatever happened, Wynnie couldn't stop caring about her mom completely. That woman had been all the family she had.

There were recent tags on her timeline, photos of a funeral. My blood chilled as I scrolled through them and realisation dawned on me.

The funeral was her mother's.

Shit.

I glanced at Wynter and tried to be strong for her but I felt like crying myself. Not over that woman but the fact that Wynnie had never gotten to say goodbye properly or been able to resolve anything.

I was about to close the app when my thumb landed on the news article from Wisconsin where some idiot had tagged Wynter's mother again. Bile rose in my throat upon finding out that she had been murdered in her home with a knife stuck to her neck. Her boyfriend, Joshua Andrews, claimed that some intruder had broken in and had gotten to his partner but he had chased them off before he himself could be harmed. He was currently under investigation.

Wynter lowered her hands and stared at me with bloodshot eyes.

"He's going to spin a tale to get himself cleared of any charges," she told me in a dead whisper. "Just like he did the last time I outed him on social media. People would believe him because he doesn't show his nasty side to anyone but those he wants to destroy."

The defeat in her tone got to me so bad, I ran my fingers through my hair in frustration and stood up, needing to pace the forest floor instead of holding her like I should. I couldn't bear it. I couldn't bear how she sounded like she had given up on ever being able to bring that monster down. She hadn't believed she could then. She didn't believe it now. His memories, his power over her pain and thoughts would never completely fade. There was no doubt in my mind either that Joshua was the one who had killed Wynter's mother, He had certainly spoken of it to her before and he was a psychopath, a sick human being from what she had told me of him. People like that weren't capable of loving someone or having a conscience.

"Do you think she missed me?" my girlfriend's soft voice penetrated my rampant thoughts. "Maybe even a little. Maybe during her last moments when she finally saw his true colours. Do you think she believed me then?"

My eyes burned with unshed tears for her. All she had wanted was to feel safe, to be believed. Her own parent couldn't do that for her but she still felt grief, still managed to love so deeply with the bruises nobody else could see.

"He finally succeeded in taking everything I had ever known from me," was her final sadly uttered statement before she stood up and gave me a blank look. "We should go pack."

Wynter

3.

I wasn't okay. It shouldn't have gutted me this way but it had. No matter what, she was still my family. Had been. I closed my eyes in pain. Had been my only family. I had run not just to protect myself but her as well. I'd spoken out about my past to the world months ago not to make Mom's life unhappy but to make my truth known even if nothing had been proven in court.

And I'd thought I'd moved on. I'd thought Joshua would be good to her once I wasn't around to serve as a distraction or become a problem. But he'd always been a little deranged and finally something must have snapped.

She'd had blonde hair like mine, a fragile body and deep down, a need for love and acceptance after my father's death. As a single mother, things hadn't been easy for her. Maybe that was why she had clung to Joshua for as long as she had.

I gritted my teeth as more pain threatened to overwhelm me. Why was I making excuses for her like this? Why was I mourning for her? Why did I feel so much rage that he'd killed her when she and I had cut off all ties a long time ago.

I had Jude, right? I was supposed to be over all this and not let anything Joshua did get to me anymore. But he was still in my head. The plague that had ruined my home life and family. A dark specter which refused to leave me alone even when I was wide awake and in a safe place. That rape play scenario with Jude had taught me just how traumatized I still was. And now this unexpected turbulence in my emotional sphere was threatening to crush me.

I hadn't pushed that knife in deep enough all those months ago in Wisconsin. I regretted it now. If I had been a little stronger, a little braver...my mother would've been alive today. I'd left her with that monster and now she was gone.

Jude's fingers entwined with mine over the console of Ella's car as we drove away from our former sanctuary an hour later. Ella was still tied up in the cabin and we had decided to tip the authorities once we were clear of the area. It still irked me how he had cupped her cheek and sounded almost sorry when he told her he was leaving and she will never see him again. Then he had reassured her that someone will come for her soon.

So good. Always so good.

He would never truly understand my thirst for revenge, to ruin people who had once tried to ruin us even if he did acknowledge the unfairness of it. Jude Knight might have followed me over to the other side but he was still strait-laced in so many ways. I had to push him over the edge in order for him to accompany me because he'd never do it by himself.

I guess there was something to be said about balance in a relationship.

"Where are we going to go this time?" I questioned him numbly as the car sped down the freeway, nothing but trees and road in my line of vision and the stirring tones of *Follow You* by Bring Me The Horizon flowing out of the speakers.

We were a long way from the next town and I was feeling so tired. That bitch Ella's intrusion had fucked up everything. I took my hand away from his as the image of him being nice to her when we departed the cabin filtered through my messed up mind yet again.

"Out of the country," Jude replied to my surprise and I had to turn to look at him to check if he was serious.

"How in hell are we-?"

"Just leave it to me," he said curtly. "We have more money than we will ever need, Wynter. I can manage getting us to another country where we don't have to hide so much and will at least be more in control of matters relating to the law. I've texted Brent and he's going to help me sort it out."

Can I go and kill that motherfucker first though? I wanted to ask but bit my tongue.

We weren't Bonnie and Clyde by a long shot. I wouldn't trade this man for anything in the world but if he could forgive Ella and treat her well after all the damage her bitchy mouth had caused him, then him allowing me to blow Joshua Andrews' brains out was something Jude would never condone.

It may be ride or die with us but he was the light to my darkness and that was how it always will be. He'd given me so much love and treated me like a fucking princess. I guess I could make myself respect his stance on certain things.

"We'll find a motel by nightfall, honey," he told me in a warmer voice this time which melted some of the ice.

Then he reached for me again and pinned our clasped hands to his thigh as if he had no intention of letting me go. Parts of him were different since we had moved away from civilization. Jude had always been protective of me and had never been afraid to speak up in my defence but nowadays, he was insanely possessive.

It made my heart flutter because it meant he was so into me that I bet if I ever disappeared from his life now, Jude would be the one to stalk me this time. He wouldn't let me go. He couldn't stay without me just like I couldn't stay without him. It was unhealthy and fucked up and yet, I wanted that. I wanted that for as long as we lived.

"I'll arrange everything for you and you'll leave in a couple of days but I won't join you right away."

The bottom seemed to drop out of my world when he said that.

"What...do you mean?" I questioned in a very slow and very careful manner. "Did I just hear you say that you *won't* be joining me right away? Why can't we both go together? I'm not leaving without you."

He clicked his tongue and slowed the car a little as the atmosphere within its confines grew tense.

"It's too risky if we leave together. And I have some business to take care of."

That was bullshit. We could make anything work if we stayed together and he knew it.

"I'm the one who organizes everything business-related for you," I reminded him. "What is suddenly so urgent that you think you need to handle it alone? I'm still your assistant in case it slipped your mind."

He let out a sigh as we rounded a bend on the road and I was thrown against the passenger door momentarily. It was still broad daylight but thankfully, we were in disguise and the plan was to abandon Ella's car in the next town then hitch a ride from there.

"*Hierchay* is being sold and they're inviting tenders so I need to finalize the deal before I leave. I want you to go before me and remain there. I need to make sure you're safe before I take care of this. Phillipa will be there with you so you won't feel alone."

Was he kidding me right now? "*When* did you decide this?" I asked sharply and snatched my hand away again because I was so angry. "You want to buy out *Hierchay*? The same firm that dumped you at your lowest? You should be glad they couldn't stay afloat after you left those assholes. And you want me to leave the fucking country while you're here finalizing a *business* deal?! What the fuck, Jude?"

"You're being dramatic. Just let me do what I have to do without having to worry about you putting yourself at risk while I'm busy."

I stared at him as his meaning washed over me. He thought I'd go after Joshua. That I wasn't going to stay put after learning of my mother's death. He knew me so fucking well. The storm inside me was brewing and looking for an outlet. And this time, my power was *not* an illusion. I would kill and I would make him suffer.

"Wynnie, please." Jude looked over at me briefly with an earnest expression on his handsome face. "I listen to you every time. I do whatever you need me to, give you whatever you ask of me. I don't even care if that makes me seem like a pussy." He frowned and his tone grew rigid and uncompromising this time. "Let me do what I need to do for us now. For once, I need you to listen to me. No arguments."

I didn't talk to him for the rest of the drive. Or even when we reached a gas station and abandoned Ella's car before calling the cops stationed nearer to where we had lived so we could inform them about her. And not even when a trucker gave us a ride at the back and we travelled like that for miles, lying on the bed of the truck and brooding.

"Just a few days, Wynnie," he spoke up first after the silence grew heavier than the weight on my chest. "I promise you won't have to run or hide anymore. We've had our blissful isolation experience and it was much needed. But you're only nineteen and I don't want that life for you. I don't want that life for myself anymore either. I'm ready to be J. R. Knight again. I'm ready to be strong with you."

I wanted to answer him but stubbornness kept me quiet. But I still appreciated that he wasn't ignoring me. That he made an effort to bridge the tiny rift between us. I trusted whatever plans he had made for the future but I also hated that he had made them without me. We were supposed to be partners in crime here. And instead of understanding my grief and desire for vengeance, he was talking about business.

By dusk, we reached a motel somewhere on the outskirts of Juneau and checked in using one of my fake IDs. Yup. I still had those lying around. Our room was the nicest one in the establishment and I was happy to have a clean, safe place to spend the night.

But when I fell asleep, I dreamed of Joshua Andrews. He was holding a knife to my throat and leering at me saying, "I will come for you, Wynnie. I will get rid of you just like I got rid of her but first..." His fingers found my panties and I tried to scream but couldn't. My mother's corpse was lying right next to us and he wanted me to look into her dead eyes while he-

"Wynter! Wake the fuck up."

I was jostled awake by Jude and pushed him away on instinct because my skin was crawling and my heart was beating so fast, I couldn't catch my breath as I buried my fingers in my hair and felt like tearing it out of my scalp. Or screaming my lungs out. I was going crazy. I really was. My hands wanted Joshua's neck and my eyes ached to watch him die. I couldn't stop thinking of my nightmare, the way he had sounded so victorious even now.

Jude stayed away from me. He knew better than to touch me when I woke up from a bad dream. I couldn't simply melt in his arms and forget what was going on inside my goddamned mind.

"Why can't we just kill him before we go?" I gritted into the silence of our motel room, into the darkness that surrounded us where words like these sounded normal.

"*Because* Wynter, we don't want to make our situation worse," he bit out in exasperation. "We're in hot water with the law as it is. Our best move will be to leave as soon as possible." He shifted and opened a bottle of water by the nightstand before handing it to me. "I doubt Ella will out us now. I saw the look on her face after we...well, after our display in the cabin. She seemed to finally have accepted that I love you and can never be with her."

I let out a scoff and gulped down the water.

"Well she better not say anything," I replied after handing the bottle back to him. "I won't hesitate to rearrange her face next time."

He exhaled roughly and I heard him dump the bottle on the night stand before going back to sleep with his back to me. I could barely make out his form but I did see enough to know he was angry and wanted me to shut up. I on the other hand was so wound up that silence was the last thing I needed tonight. He was not going to turn his back on me this easily. I wasn't going to let him.

"What's the matter, Jude? All this talk of violence and bloodshed turning your stomach? Would you like some lavender soap and fluffy blankets to comfort you?"

"Shut the fuck up," he muttered and I grinned because I was evil like that. And unlike him, I actually enjoyed it.

I reached out a foot and trailed it up his bare leg while biting my lip. Getting him to fuck me when he kept saying no was one of my favourite things to do. That inevitable moment when his resolve shattered and he gave in to the madness was one of the headiest of experiences.

"Take those boxers off, baby," I said seductively. "I want you naked and underneath me."

"Wynnie, stop fucking around. Too much has happened today and you need to take it easy."

I rolled my eyes at his sage advice and took my t-shirt off. I needed this. I always did. Especially when too much happened and there wasn't anything I could do to fix it. Taking it out on him through sex was what helped even though he tried to get me to process it in a healthier way.

He must have heard the whisper of clothes leaving my body because he said, "The walls are too thin. We can't."

My vagina was already growing moist at the scenario because I knew very well that the walls were too thin. And I didn't care. I loved fucking him and I would love it if people could hear us doing it because it was hot. And Jude might deny it all he wants but it was hot for him as well.

"Should I gag you then?" I whispered as I scooted closer to his warm body and inserted my thigh between his, giving him a nip on his shoulder.

"You're louder than I am," he replied, making me smile because it was true. But he could be loud too.

Nobody heard us back where we had lived so we'd made it a habit not to hold back in any way during sex.

"Let's make a bet," I mumbled in his ear while my hand went to his erection and massaged the length of it. "Whoever cries out first will leave the country first too. And the other one gets to stay back and take care of...business."

Jude's hand moved down to grip mine and we both spent a few seconds stroking his dick and getting him hard as a pole. "How do you want it?" he mumbled back.

I knew exactly how. Hard. Fast. Unhampered by emotion or tenderness. Just me taking his body the way I loved to. Shamelessly and with a sense of naughtiness thrown in because of the whole age difference. I relished what he became with me.

"Turn on your back," I instructed him.

Once he did, I bent to his cock and licked it with long, firm strokes of my tongue, cupped his balls and squeezed a little and then took his fingers to rub them over my clit and spread my juices over my folds.

It felt so lewd and animalistic and I liked it, the feel of his rough fingers rubbing me and then pushing in and out of me under my guidance. I was ready in no time and mounted him as though he was a prized stallion and I was the only female for miles. Yeah, I knew how mating worked with animals but Jude and I rolled differently, depending on our moods. I was the one who needed to top this time.

When I sunk onto his cock, my teeth dug into my bottom lip at the sensation, the feeling of being filled up and at home, the nerve-endings which were set alight at that first physical contact of his heavy length inside me.

"You're such a bad boy," I whispered in the dark and he pumped into me in response because he secretly enjoyed it when I called him those dirty, degrading things.

I was the only girl in this world for whom Jude Reginald Knight would sink to his knees and that was my power. I was not ashamed to admit that. It was only fair since he had me so hooked on him that I almost went insane at the thought of us ever separating.

Pressing my palms to his chest, I began to rock my hips, increasing my pace little by little and gasping as my blood heated and pulse raced. I clenched around him as I rode him fiercely but he was stubbornly silent. The only indication that I drove him wild was the vice-like grip he had on my hips.

"Come on," I urged and bounced on his cock so hard, the bed started to creak. "I know you want to scream for me, baby. Do it. Feel that lovely, young pussy that's dripping just for you. Because it can't get enough of your huge-"

I was stunned when he suddenly lifted me off him and tossed me on the bed face down like he sometimes does when he feels like dominating. And then his head was between my thighs, lapping up the moisture with his tongue and spreading me out almost crudely while I braced myself on my elbows and watched him, unable to make out much.

Pleasure ripped through me as his mouth worked on me down there, the way he was licking me with confident, dragged out swipes of his tongue.

"Jude," I whispered and my hand reached behind me to grip his hair while I tried not to growl at him. "Fuck, that's so good."

He lifted his head and again, I found myself being shifted until my ass was in the air and my face pushed against the mattress. I was enjoying his roughness and take-charge attitude so much, I was grinning into the sheets, my hair plastered to my face due to the sweat I had worked up.

"What about this? Is this good?" he asked me and fingered my back hole.

I'd already taken him in there countless times but it still felt naughty.

"Uh-huh. But your dick will be even better," I told him and he lubed me up with my own pussy juice before gripping my hips and pushing inside me.

I groaned when he slid in but Jude remained absolutely silent except for a low hiss. It was maddening. I was supposed to be making him scream.

"Oh god," I said and muffled my voice into the mattress as pleasure spread all across my body.

My fingers went to my clit and rubbed furiously while he fucked me and also buried two digits inside my vagina for good measure.

"Jesus," I said, my eyes rolling with sensation.

"You want to say that a little louder, baby?" he asked in a strained voice. "You wanted people to hear us, right? So let them," he jerked out and thrusted hard once.

So hard, a sharp cry exited my mouth. I couldn't help it. That was unfair. He meant for that to happen so I would lose. Motherfucker.

And once he had won the bet, he stopped playing games and gave himself over to the tide of pleasurable sensations and overwhelming lust. I let him take me the way he wanted and we both didn't bother to stifle our moans as we came hard in the end.

Jude took me in his arms afterwards, kissed my hair and rubbed my shoulders absently while I tucked myself into his side and went to sleep, the torment I was in earlier fading away for the rest of the night.

But I knew by now that running away from the big, bad things that haunted us was not a long-term solution. The nightmares would come back. As long as I ran, I would remain a little bit broken. I hadn't been strong enough to exact vengeance for myself. And I was helpless to do it now for my mother. I only wished I could live with myself and with Jude for cowering from what needed to be done this time around.

Jude

4.

Saying goodbye to Wynter was the hardest thing. She was all wide-eyed and baby-faced. Her fingers clung to mine until the very end when it was time to board the private jet I had chartered for this trip. And the way she pressed her mouth to mine before drawing back and saying, "You better come back to me, Mr. Knight, or I swear there will be hell to pay," nearly broke my resolve.

I steeled myself against the misery and angst, the clawing need to drop all other commitments and take her in my arms again so we could fly out together. This girl had so much power over me that the idea of separation felt like drilling a hole in my chest.

"Be safe, baby," I whispered as I watched the jet take off an hour later and pulled my hat down low over my face before heading over to the other side of the airport where my own private plane was waiting.

It bothered me now that my life had turned into this cat and mouse game. That I had become so weak I'd chosen the easy way out. The coward's way out. Months ago, for the sake of our mental health, it had been the wisest course. But who was I kidding? I'd seen the way Wynnie had enjoyed her short-lived friendship with Brent's daughter. I'd taken such simple things away from her and wrapped us in a fantasy that was neither practical nor healthy for a teenage girl.

Sometimes, it felt like those other people had been right, like they'd been justified in hating me because I was a groomer. I'd given in to the wiles of a young fan by letting her stay in my house and then sleeping with her. It didn't matter that she'd already been obsessed or that she'd lied about her age. Even when I had found out the truth, I'd played a huge role in taking our relationship to where it was today.

I was a sick bastard, yes. But I did love her. So much that if I didn't do this one thing for her, I knew I would regret it for the rest of my life.

Buying out *Hierchay* was not a lie. But it was an excuse. For what, I never intended for her to know.

Wynter

5.

France. He'd decided to bring us to France. I had never even set foot out of the country before but here I was lounging on a villa near the coast with a drink in my hand, watching the sunset. It was a strange experience for me. We weren't exactly in the clear just because we had moved to another country. Jude was still well-known and the danger of being discovered would surround us at every turn but for now, nobody in the world except for Brent and Phillipa knew our exact location. And this time, I hoped Ella wouldn't interfere and leave us the hell alone for good.

But it had been almost forty-eight hours so a tiny sliver of doubt began to creep into my heart that maybe Jude had changed his mind about me. Maybe he had decided to wash his hands off the mess that was Wynter Cassidy and use his money and power to clear himself of all charges and brave the public this time.

He was different now. Tougher. He didn't need me, right? Ella would help him. They might even be planning to be together.

My fingers clutched at the glass I was holding as sunlight streamed into my eyes and I got off the lounger to walk over to the balcony and peer at the sparkling ocean right below.

What if he doesn't come back?

He hadn't called me. Hadn't even texted. I'm supposed to be mad at him but I'm worried and I can't sleep at nights. All this distance for what? A business deal?

It couldn't be that simple. Not with a man like Jude.

"He'll be back soon, Wynter."

Phillipa's voice carried across the patio from behind me and I whirled to regard her angrily, no longer able to keep the panic from my voice.

"So he has spoken to you?" I demanded shrilly and felt like hurling the glass into her calm face because Jude Knight made me want to do psychotic shit like that. Why would he speak to her and not me? What the hell was going on?

"He only said he needed more time and I could return once he joined you here," Phillipa told me gravely. "Let him do what needs to be done, girl."

I stared daggers at her and hated myself for it because I actually liked Phillipa and she was only trying to help us while risking getting in trouble with the law. I should be thanking her for it, not resenting her.

Reluctantly, I headed inside the villa which I also resented because I missed our fucking cabin. That warm, secluded place which had kept Jude occupied with nothing but me and his writing. *That* was how I had wanted to live. I needed him to only think of me and nobody else, nothing else, although I did understand his passion for writing. It was the exception to my rule and the only other thing that made him happy so I wasn't going to take that away from him.

But as soon as the real world interfered, life became messy and complicated. Fucking miserable.

I just wanted him back.

Phillipa tried to stop me from drinking but I think even she wasn't sure I would refrain from harming her so she went into the other room and bade me goodnight.

I hated wine. Absolutely hated it. But I made myself gulp it down because my sobriety was torture right now. I missed him more than anyone should be allowed to miss someone. And I was grieving for Mom so that made this separation a thousand times worse.

"I hate you," I slurred into the pillow as the wine bottle fell from my limp fingers a couple of hours later. "I hate you, Jude. It's not okay if you leave me. It's not okay because I *can't* live without you and you know that. So please...for the love of God...just come back to me."

Jude

6.

There was blood on my clothes. Sticky, reeking blood which hurt me to look at and made me nauseous. I'd wanted it to be clean. I'd planned for it to be over quickly, to catch him unawares and then be out of there before his body had collapsed to the floor.

But death wasn't clean. *Killing someone* wasn't clean. He hadn't gone down easy. I'd waited until it was nightfall to sneak inside his house and off him in his sleep but like the clumsy amateur I was, I'd ended up stubbing my toe against the bottom of the couch and sending the lamp crashing to the floor. He'd woken up as I'd winced, immediately seen the gun in my hands and lurched towards it. Just as he'd clutched my wrist, I had fired the shot but he had been big and strong and his pudgy fingers had wrapped themselves around my throat, trying to squeeze the life out of me.

Recognition had lit up his eyes a few seconds in and he had sneered at me.

"She sent you to finish me off, did she?" he had growled, bleeding out but not easing up on his grip. "I knew she wouldn't be able to help herself after finding out what I did to her mother. She used to let me behave however I wanted with her just to keep that bitch of her mum safe."

My vision had started to blacken and the gun dropped from my hands before I clutched the back of his hand with my fingers, trying to pry it off my neck. I had to get back to Wynnie. I promised her I would. It couldn't end like this.

"Where is she?" Joshua demanded wheezily, his eyes wild with some kind of perverted excitement I couldn't even decipher. "Where is my little girl? I know all about the two of you." He grimaced and shook me a little. "She couldn't give that ass to me but she can give it to you? I took care of her. I was her daddy. You know what it's like, right? You know how the young ones are with their horny little pussies. I barely waited for her to grow up."

I swear if I hadn't been struggling to catch my breath, I would have thrown up in his face because of the way he was talking about her but instead, I let go of his wrist and dug my fingers roughly into his gunshot wound.

Joshua let out a howl and I used the brief moment of distraction to ram my fist into his face before shoving him away from me. I couldn't breathe for some time as I fell to my hands and knees but I couldn't afford the luxury of recovering either. He would kill me and I would never see her face again. Even in my death, Wynter would never forgive me for this.

With a shaking hand, I lifted the gun once more and aimed it at him where he had collapsed next to the couch, finally weakened by the wound I had inflicted.

Joshua's eyes narrowed at me, his breathing growing labored as we regarded each other with hatred. How on earth had she faced him back then and survived? This man was not an easy opponent. His strength had been considerable. This was the predator who had made her life a living hell for two complete years before trying to rape her. This was the monster who had instilled so much fear in her and ripped away a safety she had been entitled to in such a way that she still had nightmares because of it. That she sometimes even looked at me as if I would turn into a Joshua and hurt her the same way. The man who had haunted her long enough.

No more now, Wynnie, I thought to myself. *No more.*

My heart ached for her so much and even more so when he grinned at me and said, "Killing me...isn't going to bring her mother back. My death...will never mean...her victory."

I shut him up before he said anything else which would make me abandon all my efforts to get this over with quickly and subject him to a very slow and excruciatingly painful demise.

I'd done the right thing, I told myself, as I made sure I left no evidence behind before exiting the house. All I wanted was to get as far away from there as possible and not think about what I had done. It would have been easier to hire somebody else to do the dirty work but it also would have been cowardly.

This was for her. This was all for her because nobody had ever protected her before. Not the law, not her mother, not her friend.

Her *friend*. Yeah, I hadn't been able to talk myself into killing a teenage boy because I had hoped he would learn from his mistakes. But it had been so easy to lure him into that shed in the woods when I had told him about the money I was willing to pay to watch him have sex with another girl out there. An unconscious girl.

That sick piece of shit. He hadn't learned his lesson at all even after being exposed months ago. He had shown up.

Well, he wasn't going to be showing up anywhere else for a couple of days while he stayed locked up in that dark shed, tied to a chair and blindfolded. It was amazing how much power a gun could hold. I hadn't let him see my face or answered him when he had asked me what I was doing. I'd just left him there.

It wasn't a fit punishment but it would definitely make him think twice in future about accepting such deals. At least, I hoped so. To me, Noah just seemed like another Joshua in the making.

I gave myself three days. Three days to cleanse my soul of any guilt and tell myself to man up and let it go. I would do anything for Wynter. If it meant shooting down every fucker who tries to harm her one by one, I would do it. I would fucking do it because I knew she would do the same for me. We had each other's backs. Always.

Wynter

7.

One morning that same week, I came out of the bathroom and thought maybe I had started hallucinating. On the other side of the wide glass doors of my bedroom, there was Jude, lounging out on the patio with Phillipa and Brent, having a laugh over drinks.

I stood there with my gaze pinned on the three of them and wished I had laser vision or something so it could sear through the glass and my point would be made. I didn't even care when he had arrived. All I knew was that he hadn't tried to see me first. How hard was it to hop inside the bathroom? Instead, he was out there with his friends having a good time while I stewed in my misery.

But then I paused and really looked at him.

He was having a good time with his friends.

When was the last time that had happened?

Brent had only visited us once every two months and never stayed long for fear of discovery. He had a family to think about. But now, everything felt normal. Jude was normal.

And maybe normal wasn't so bad, the voice inside me piped up.

I sniffed and flopped down on the bed before picking up a bottle of moisturizer, dabbing some on my legs and proceeding to smooth it over my skin.

"It is if he keeps ignoring me," I muttered as I continued with my task.

Every cell in my body screamed for me to go and haul myself at him now that he was here but I made myself stay put. I hero-worshipped this guy but right now, it felt as if he didn't deserve my desperation. Maybe my resentment arose from the fact that I had been the center of his attention for so long and now I wasn't.

After putting on a pair of shorts and a cotton t-shirt, I went downstairs and took the longer route to the beach below.

I honestly couldn't get enough of it. In my town in Wisconsin, I'd only gotten a chance to go to the beach a few times in my life and then never once in Alaska. Jude had told me we would travel the world once things quietened down but we had been so engrossed in each other and the sweet seclusion that we never ventured out of state.

So the beach was getting most of my attention now. Better than *him*. I wasn't going to throw myself at his feet either if the prospect of seeing me after our first separation in months didn't affect him at all.

Was he falling out of love with me? Was that it?

"I think you're the only girl in the world who actually manages to make sadness look almost appealing," a deep voice said from behind me as I stood at the edge of the water and stared out at the ocean.

A light snort escaped my throat. I didn't turn around to see who had spoken. I'd seen him a couple of times talking walks on the beach with his guitar and once he had sat at the foot of a tree on shore and sang in such a beautiful, haunting voice.

He was probably around my age, really good-looking with the body of an athlete, toned and bronzed. I couldn't place his origin. Middle Eastern? Italian? He looked like one and sounded like the other. I'd also noticed him watching me whenever I came out here but he had never approached me till now.

"That's a very strange compliment," I replied dryly as warm, subtle beach waves teased my feet. My heart was *aching*. Jude's behaviour was rotting up my insides and I hated the helplessness so much.

"An honest one though," the boy replied. I heard him strumming his guitar and when he sang several lines of a song I really liked, my eyes filled with tears.

"Who are you and what do you want from me?" I questioned the guy wearily, ready to send him on his way if he tried to make a pass. He was wasting his time.

"My name's Ziad," he answered, moving closer to stand beside me. "But my friends call me Zi. Just travelling through and I couldn't help but notice how sad you look all the time. Want to talk about it?"

I glanced at his face then and couldn't even speak for a moment. He was...pretty hot. I didn't think I had ever looked at a guy apart from Jude and actually been this awed by his beauty.

"What's in it for you?" I asked suspiciously.

He laughed a little, running a free hand through his hair. "Wow. Why does everyone keep asking me that? Can't a guy just be nice to someone without having an ulterior motive?"

His question immediately made me think of Jude and I stifled the smile that threatened to curve my lips. No, damn it. I was mad at him!

"Please tell me that is your older brother or a *very* close relative," Ziad said to me ruefully and I followed his gaze to the balcony of my new home.

My chest squeezed painfully when I noticed Jude standing there, peering down at us. He was alone. Brent and Phillipa must have left. I forced myself to look away. So now he suddenly remembers I exist?

"That's um...that's not my brother," I mumbled, frowning down at my feet.

Ziad made a regretful noise. "Damn. Why are all the good ones always taken?" he moaned and even though he acted casual, I detected something more in his tone. Something like real hurt.

"I'm not good, trust me." My mouth twisted in a snarky smile. "You're better off."

Again, he laughed. A melodious sound. Everything about him was gorgeous. What was he doing coming up to a sad girl like me? I bet he had females falling all over him wherever he went.

"You do this professionally?" I asked, gesturing at his guitar.

He shrugged in response. "A few gigs here and there. I like to keep myself guessing. Be undecided about things. Adds more spice to life."

I smiled warmly then because I kind of agreed with him.

"Oh, shit," he muttered and I caught him glancing behind me a little warily. "He's coming down. Is he the jealous and aggressive type? I kind of like my face."

A sigh escaped me because apart from that one time when his friend William had touched me and Jude had lost his shit in public, he had never gotten jealous. Hell, even then his reaction had been less due to jealousy and more out of a sense of protectiveness he must have felt towards his young 'assistant'.

"You're safe. He wouldn't hurt a fly," I told my unexpectedly charming companion.

After Noah's betrayal, I had never bothered to build any lasting friendships but talking to Ziad made me feel a little hopeful. Maybe he really was nice. Not everyone had to be a Noah. It was hard to get over my trust issues though. They'd all been nice to me in the beginning before turning around and stabbing me in the back.

"It was nice meeting you, Zi."

He gave me a surprised look. "Whoa. I'm being dismissed? He's *that* important?"

I didn't answer but he probably read it on my face and smiled kindly.

"Don't let him make you sad," the boy told me and started to back off. "Oh and I'll be around for a few more weeks in case you ever do feel like talking."

With a slight wave at me and another glance at Jude, he walked off, leaving me with a pleasant feeling in my heart. I wondered if he truly was just that sort of guy. Someone who simply wanted to make others feel better. That was some rare shit in this fucked up world.

"Wyn?"

I closed my eyes and refused to look at him. My instincts wanted me to clutch at him, feel him straining against me until there wasn't an inch of space between us anymore and hurt him a little to vent my frustration but I stubbornly remained silent. Even when he came up behind me and put his hands on my hips, squeezing a little and even when he dipped his head to suck on the side of my neck. Already he was growing hard against me, I felt it nudging my ass and then gasped a little when his hands moved under my t-shirt possessively and cupped my bare breasts, his thumbs brushing against my nipples.

"I'm mad at you," I managed to choke out as I began to grow wet and my body heated up from the way he was so blatantly feeling me up in public.

This wasn't a private beach. Anyone walking by could see us. Zi was probably looking at us right now.

"Well can you be mad at me and fuck me at the same time because I can't wait?" Jude said to me in a rough voice and moved abruptly to drag me with him towards the water.

What in the world was he doing?

In the ocean?

"Did I tell you sex on the beach made it to my bucket list back when we were in Florida?" he asked me casually as I followed him into the water, mesmerized by his attitude. "Sex in the ocean however sounds much better."

Every time this man used the word 'sex', he made it sound so dirty and appealing, I grew breathless trying to figure out just how he managed to nail it.

Once we were about waist deep, he turned to face me. The sun's rays were behind him and I remained in his shadow as we watched each other. He'd taught me how to swim in the river back at the cabin and I was grateful because this was probably going to be a challenge.

I studied his face as his fingers went to my shorts and he worked on removing them. His eyes had dark circles underneath, the only indication that he hadn't slept well these past few nights either. I wondered if it was because he had missed me or because...

No. Jude wouldn't do that to me. He wouldn't cheat. Not on me.

But the man wouldn't meet my eyes properly and that bothered me. Warm water lapped at our bodies as I moved closer to him, feeling his heat and knowing that the ocean wasn't the only thing responsible for making me wet.

"Why didn't you call me? Why did you switch your phone off?" I asked and bit back a moan when his hand dipped inside the opening of my shorts and his fingers stroked my clit.

Despite the sounds of the ocean, I heard him drag in a breath through his teeth as his eyes grew hooded, the blue in them more pronounced than ever.

"Take my cock out," was his response and it wasn't even a question whether I obeyed him or not.

Of course I took it out. It felt so smooth and rock-hard, glistening as the water covered it. The thrill I experienced crashed all my doubts and questions for the time being. My pussy had missed being pounded by this thing and I just wanted it in me.

Jude dragged my shorts down and I eagerly helped him, feeling more than a little naughty.

"Can I show my boobs too?" I asked him, suddenly starting to enjoy this immensely.

His sexy mouth quirked a little and he winked at me. "Sure. Knock yourself out."

My answering smirk couldn't be helped. I loved this new, bolder side of him. He had always been bold in private but in public? This was hot.

So I didn't think twice before whipping my wet t-shirt off and tossing it in the water. It was his turn as he undressed and my eyes widened because I still couldn't quite believe Jude Knight was going to do this. It hadn't mattered in Alaska but we didn't have the luxury of isolation and privacy anymore. With Ella, I had tempted him into it. I'd tempted and seduced him into a lot of things.

This was a first.

When he was finally as naked as me and took me in his arms, I let myself moan out loud at the heavenly feel of his body against mine. At the sparse but sexy as fuck hair on his muscular chest which made him so much a man and the strength with which he held me, his wet, warm mouth latching on to a nipple and sucking gently.

I pulled his head up by the hair and kissed that mouth, stabbing my tongue in and grinding against him. Jude's hands grabbed my ass as one leg of mine went around his hips while I balanced on the other.

"Mm-hm." He broke the kiss and shook his head, his erection poking at me. "Both legs. I want you wrapped around me."

I wanted that too. So much. So I did as he asked, the water helping to keep me afloat, making the added weight easier on him. My tits were crushed against his chest and we weren't hidden from the waist up so I instinctively looked around but he held my chin between his thumb and forefinger and made me focus on him.

"Look at me while I'm fucking you," he commanded in a deep voice and that first plunge of his cock inside me made me go crazy.

"Oh, god." I whined at the searing pleasure as he slid me up and down his shaft and my movements started to become frenzied. I missed this so fucking bad. I didn't want to go slow.

The water splashed lightly around us as I chased that orgasm and kept my eyes on his, the enjoyment and love visible in both our expressions.

"That boy," I gasped suddenly as he bounced me on his cock, gripping my ass hard. "When you saw me with him...you didn't feel jealous?"

Jude breathed out a laugh before groaning a little as I clenched around him. "Not even for a second," he replied lazily.

I frowned then, my pace slowing down a bit even as my body cried out for a release. "Why not?" I wanted to know, feeling more than a little disappointed with his answer.

I kind of wanted him to go alpha male on me and demand I never talk to another guy again. Every girl wanted that sometimes, right? But Jude never-

"Because I know you're obsessed with me," the son of a bitch answered and bit my neck as he thrusted inside me.

I clenched my jaw at that statement. He didn't sound arrogant or entitled to my affections otherwise I would have climbed off his unfairly hot body and left him to jerk off here in the ocean. He just sounded like it was a fact that was unchangeable. Like the sky was blue and the earth was round and the sun arose every day. Just like that, Wynter Cassidy was obsessed with J. R. Knight.

"Obsession fades, you know," I quipped smartly and turned my face away from his. I didn't have to look at him in order to enjoy his impressive cock.

That was when he did something that shocked the sass out of me. His hand came up to grip my throat while I clutched at his shoulders to stay upright. I was forced to meet his gaze then and I saw a madness there that I only ever found in myself. The look that didn't give a damn about what was right and normal and proper when it came to us.

"Yours won't," he told me in a cold voice.

No. Not told. He *warned* me. That was most definitely a cloaked warning. Like I better not give up on him or else... I swallowed and he must have felt it against his fingers because he relaxed his grip.

Damned if his dangerous attitude didn't make my pussy even more wet and make me want to ravish him. This was a side of him that I was fast starting to get attached to just like I had gotten attached to other sides of him. Something was different about him and I wasn't complaining.

"Fuck me harder," I told him urgently.

He did, making me moan deeply. I leaned in to bite him on the corner of his lips and started to laugh a little. I wished people could see us now. Just how we were with each other. Look at us. Envy us.

"I'm close," I breathed out, riding him for all he was worth and he growled in response.

We gasped and finished a few seconds later, the climax intense and satisfying. For now.

He didn't let me go straight away. The gentle lapping of the water and the aftermath of my orgasm was peaceful and comforting. I still wanted some answers but at that moment, I was content to stay in my lover's embrace.

It got chilly in the afternoon. Weirdly enough, this house was loosely modeled after Jude's old apartment in Atlanta with hues of soft grey and black and splashes of white thrown in. I liked the ambience a lot. It was modern, sleek but somehow still cozy and comfortable. One wall was completely made up of glass and faced the ocean. The sky outside was gray now while I remained huddled in a sofa in my jeans and a sweater, with fuzzy slippers, cradling a cup of coffee in my hands as I watched Jude at the kitchen counter, typing something on his laptop.

He was shirtless, freshly showered and just in sweats with strands of his hair falling endearingly over his intelligent brow. Damn. Could he be any hotter? And so smart, mature and confident. It was like anyone could throw anything at this guy now and he wouldn't bat an eye. He was starting to give off some serious mafia vibes. But with the nerdiness to go with it which just made him an even greater package.

Okay, Wynnie. Seriously. Stop fucking mooning over him and get to the tough part.

I sighed and took a small sip of the coffee before speaking up firmly.

"I have questions."

He lifted his head from his task, paused for a moment to study my expression and then looked back at the screen.

"Go ahead and ask them. I really haven't slept well these past few nights and I need to tonight. I know it's going to keep you up and then you'll keep me up as well so let's get it over with."

I should have written them down or something because he was right. We had fucked and I was calmer now but when night fell and he slept next to me, I'd be the restless one who tasted bad dreams and dealt with insecurities.

"When did you buy this house?"

I knew it hadn't been a last minute purchase given the thought that had gone into its design.

"Last month," he answered, the tap, tap, tap of the keyboard never ceasing as he talked. "I'd been wanting to have a back-up for some time but last month, I looked it up and decided on this one. Phillipa came and took a look at it for me, set things up. Never imagined we would have to move so quickly though but I'm glad I was prepared."

I nodded at the explanation, feeling slightly resentful that he hadn't told me but still understanding his reasoning. Jude hadn't wanted me to worry. We'd been living such a good life there and mentions of moving away or being discovered would have soured up my mood and made me fret unnecessarily. As I digested that news, I realized I was actually pretty grateful that he had planned this in advance for both our future and safety. Something to be said about older guys though not all of them thought this way. I was fortunate, I guess.

"Fair enough," I conceded and sipped some more coffee.

"Anything else?" he murmured, scratching his chin while frowning at the screen, probably documenting some ideas in case he never heard from them again.

"Oh, yes, there's plenty more," I replied and put my coffee aside. "I'm not done by a long shot, J. R. Knight."

His lips quirked a little at my term of address before he resumed his serious typing. He loved that, didn't he? He never really wanted to be parted from that identity. He just hadn't wanted it to consume him.

"So why didn't you try to contact me and blocked me from contacting you?" was my next question which was difficult for me to voice because he had avoided it in the ocean and I had a feeling I wasn't going to like the answer.

"Baby, I told you. I needed to take care of business," he replied in a maddeningly robotic voice. "If I had stayed in touch, I would have felt like rushing back to you and nothing would have been accomplished. You know that. You know I wouldn't have been able to listen to your voice or see you and not drop everything to come to you." He gave me a sober look, an apologetic one. "Phillipa was here and she kept me updated so I knew you were safe. It was hell for me too, okay."

I scoffed at that because I couldn't help it.

"It was hell for you? But you still didn't bother to get in touch because what? I was a distraction? Come on, Jude. You stayed back for *Hierchay*. The same fucking firm that kicked you when you were already down. Why buy it at all? You can have your own publishing firm now. Was *Hierchay* really worth leaving me behind for?" My eyes filled up with tears unexpectedly as repressed emotions from the past several days bubbled up. "You could have gone *after* we had settled in here. I just lost my..." I paused and drew in a shaky breath. "I needed you. You were all I knew for months and suddenly you thrust me in a foreign country and don't even bother to send me one fucking text."

Jude regarded me with a pained expression for a long moment before he stood up and came over to me, his clean soapy scent washing over me as he knelt at my feet and took my face between his warm hands.

"Wynter, I promise. This is the last time," he told me with sincerity hanging from his every syllable and a gravity in his eyes. "Never again am I going to leave you, do you hear me? What needed to be done was important. I had to be fully present. But I'm here now and I swear that there will not be a repeat of this. Not unless death takes me from you."

I curled my fingers around his strong wrists and leaned forward slowly to rest my forehead against his, our warm breaths mingling and eyes shining. It hurt to love him this much sometimes. It really hurt.

"Jude," I whispered unsteadily and sniffed. "I...I hope you mean that. Because...you are...so important to me. You're everything. It feels like...you're not separate from me sometimes. Like you're in my blood and if...if I ever cut myself...I'll bleed you."

It was a struggle to articulate my emotions but he understood, I think, because he pressed a hard kiss to my mouth and then crushed me to himself, my head on his shoulder and his arms tight around me until breathing became a chore but I didn't even care. My tears were abundant as he put his lips to my hair and breathed in deeply, not letting me go for a long time.

"There were young writers employed by *Hierchay* who would have lost a lot if the firm hadn't survived," he said after a minute "People I had known and helped and given advice to when they first joined. I know they didn't support me when things blew up but they didn't actively ostracize me either. They just stayed out of the whole mess and I can understand that. *Hierchay* was everything to me, Wyn, for so many years. I don't give a fuck about the bosses, they can go to hell. But the company is mine now. I intend to register it as an imprint of *Ride or Die* publications."

I sucked in a breath and drew back from him and he let me go abruptly so I could stare at his face.

"*Ride or Die* publications?" I questioned. "When the fuck did *that* happen?"

Her smiled at me sweetly and shrugged. "I was going to tell you on your twentieth birthday. You get to manage all of it. I'll train you. Phillipa will too. We'll be unstoppable, Wynnie. We're going to build an empire upon the ashes of our past and no one is going to stand in our way. I won't let them."

God, I was so proud of him and yet, I wished he wouldn't be so sweet. Buying out *Hierchay* for those other writers and for sentimental value. Gifting me a whole fucking company. Going to such lengths to be good to people. To build an empire, sometimes you had to play it evil. Yeah he had money and power and was basically untouchable now thanks to his connections and preventative measures but he was still too nice. Too forgiving. I just got scared sometimes that that could be his downfall once more. Jude couldn't be tough when it was necessary or hurt people even when they deserved it.

"I love you," I told him and caressed his cheek, smiling at him affectionately. "Don't worry, baby. If it does get to be too much, if there is ever any danger that someone will try to stand in our way, I will fight for us. For you. You can still be a softie and I'll be the tough bitch."

Who still freaks out at the appearance of a knife in the bedroom and wakes up from nightmares that would haunt her forever. Who still suffers through the ache of regret every single moment she is alive that she could never destroy the man who disrupted her adolescence. Who will try hard every day to crush that fraction of resentment she feels towards the man who means the world to her because he didn't let her do that one thing she needed to get done because he was too...afraid.

"I love you too," he said, smiling back at me and dropping one last kiss on my mouth before standing up and going back to the kitchen, not even aware of how guilty I felt about thinking those thoughts about him. No one was perfect. I wasn't going to hold this against him. Not against my Jude.

He played a song on the sound system. *On Fire* by Andy Bumuntu. It was one of my favourites because it reminded me of Jude and the way he felt about me. Opening the sliding glass doors a fraction, he strolled outside then, running both his hands through his hair as he lifted his head and breathed in the chilly wind coming in from the sea while I huddled further in the warmth of the sofa and watched the muscles rippling across his back, those sweats complementing his powerful legs and taut buttocks.

I wanted to holler at him to come inside because he could catch cold but he moved further out to the edge of the balcony and seemed to be peering at the ocean below. Thinking of building his empire from a pile of ashes which weren't really ashes, were they? But I let him feel hopeful and optimistic because that was his dream and I didn't want to ruin it with my baggage. It was okay. I loved him. I was always going to love him to bits. Nothing would change that for me.

With a heavy heart, I reached for my phone and logged online, going immediately to Google to search up on any latest news about the murder of Diane Cassidy, the woman who had raised me. Monsters never truly went away but I kept hoping that maybe the police had found him guilty after all and sentenced him.

My feed flooded with news from my town regarding murders and I froze after a few seconds of scrolling, my fingers clutching the phone tightly when I realized that it wasn't about Diane Cassidy this time.

It was Joshua Andrews. He was found dead in my former home with two bullet holes in his chest.

I was so shocked that I didn't even know how to react for a few minutes. This was a dream. It couldn't be that easy. Fate wasn't that benevolent.

There was no way I could have everything I wanted happen exactly as I wanted it and be able to boast of a perfect life, a perfect future which I had no doubt was going to be beautiful now. Karma had finally served a cold one to Joshua fucking Andrews.

As a trickle of relief started to flow through my chest while I digested this new revelation, another alert caught my eye about Noah Harris being found after he was reported missing for forty-eight hours. Found in some cabin in the woods right near where I lived. He had no statement to make but there was a leaked video footage of him not having a stitch of clothing on his body as he was escorted by the police. The guy was hiding his face and looked like he was trying hard not to cry.

My jaw dropped and I lifted my head from the phone to look outside the glass doors once more at the man standing out there, now having turned to face me as he braced his elbows on the balcony and leaned against it.

He had been smiling faintly until he noted my expression. Everything, my deepest, most raw emotions were there for him to see on my face.

What had he done?

I didn't have to ask a single damned stupid question anymore. I didn't have to make sure or doubt what I knew to be true for even a slight moment.

I want to kill him

Just let me do what I have to do without worrying about you putting yourself at risk while I'm busy.

What needed to be done was important.

We're going to build an empire upon the ashes of our past...

My throat felt tight as I swallowed. Jude Reginald Knight. Had I been the one to say that that name didn't sound majestic?

He was no longer the man I had fallen for over a year ago. He had morphed into someone...something...even I could not fathom anymore. A figure larger than life. Too big for this world.

Too much for this world.

And here I was thinking that perfection didn't exist. I couldn't have been more wrong about him. There was not a single thing I could claim that this man had not given me now. Love like his was...

Infinite.

'Thank you,' I mouthed across the distance and his brow furrowed as he focused on what I was saying before his eyes went to the phone in my hands.

Those two words fell short of what I was experiencing, didn't even do him justice. But *he* was the master of spinning magical words together, not me. All I had were my bubbling emotions which he just seemed to get from the beginning.

Just like he was getting it now. A brief, intense look and tiny nod of acknowledgment was all he gave me before he blinked and turned away, returning his attention to the ocean once more.

He didn't do it for my thanks or to impress me. He never would have brought it up.

That had simply been something Jude needed to do for Wynter and that was it. He'd crumbled all my nightmares to dust with hands I never believed could be so powerful.

Hell yeah, we were going to build that empire. A not so obvious knight and a girl obsessed with his quiet heroism forever.

I shook my head in awe and disbelief.

Out of all the people he could have been gifted to in the whole world, he was given to me and how freaking amazing was that?

Jude

8.

Growling filthy, coarse words in Wynter's ear during sex was one of my favourite things to do while getting my dick wet. The feeling of plunging in and out of her pussy, so snug and slick topped everything of course.

She'd been right a long time ago. I liked the fact that she was kind of young for me. That this was supposed to be wrong. That being older and more mature, I should not have gotten intimately involved with a besotted fan but I'd been so tempted, so out of my fucking mind with an almost obsessive lust that I hadn't been able to help myself.

The thought fueled me. The dirty, very inappropriate and slightly disturbing thought. It didn't help that she'd done that sexy little dance for me earlier out on the balcony, rubbing her body against mine and convincing me to fuck her a couple more times before I finally got some sleep. Stars burst behind my eyelids as I released my cum inside her and let out a heavy groan, balls deep in her warmth with my forearms squeezing her breasts and teeth biting hard into the back of her neck.

"Fuck," I gasped as she milked me dry and kept pushing her ass against me, seeking more of what I'd just given her. That was the beauty of it. She craved this wild abandonment just as much as I did. "Fuck, baby. That was incredible."

We collapsed on the mattress, sweaty and exhausted for the moment. The languid feeling I experienced put an indolent smile on my face and when I had recovered a little, I pushed her hair away from her cheeks and kissed her softly, little pecks of affection which caused her to hum in satisfaction and bring her hand around to caress my jaw.

"More, please," she murmured lazily and I chuckled and rolled off her, pulling out abruptly and causing a little noise of disappointment to escape her mouth.

"Give me a minute," I said, raising one knee and running a hand through my hair as I looked up at the ceiling.

She turned over on her back as well and let out a contented sigh. At least, I believed it was contented. She certainly seemed lighter. Happier.

"Are you okay?" she asked me after a while.

I knew what she meant. I hadn't wanted her to know about my involvement in Joshua's murder and Noah's two day vacation in the forest but she'd obviously figured it out and now looked at me like I was the king of the world. I mean, she had always looked at me that way but it was way more pronounced and frequent now.

That pleased me a lot. I liked being her hero for once.

And I didn't give a fuck about the aftereffect. I had dealt with that shit back in America, had no regrets and made sure to cover my tracks well. She didn't need to worry about me. Those fuckers had deserved every inch of what I had handed them and Wynnie had deserved the closure.

"I love you," I told her and entwined my fingers with hers, the soft light of our bedroom lulling me to sleep along with the new and welcoming sound of the ocean outside. "And I'm okay, Wyn. I've never felt better, actually."

Out of my peripheral vision, I noticed her turn to me before she gasped suddenly and sat up to splay her palm on my inner thigh, gaping at the small 'Wynnie' tattoo there which I had gotten just yesterday.

"Jude," she whispered and glanced at me. "Seriously? Why am I just seeing this? A matching tat?" She laughed and leaned forward to kiss it just like I had done to hers when she'd found my name worthy enough to be permanently etched on her skin. "God...I want to ride you like a freight train after seeing this. It's turning me on like crazy."

Just her candidly spoken words made my cock stir a little and she stroked it with one finger, teasing it up and down the length and smirking at me. She looked so beautiful, naked with her just-fucked hair and skin, a happy smile on her face and her eyes shining slightly in the bedroom lights.

"Go on then," I invited as I began to harden under her touch and put my hands behind my head, giving myself over to her. "Ride your dirty old man's dick, baby. Show me some of that tight, young pussy magic."

I grinned when she got a horny expression in her eyes and bit her lip like she wanted to ravish me. I knew I was in for one hell of a ride.

"Jude," she croaked emotionally and straddled me. "I love you so fucking much. Sometimes my little heart can't even contain it. It feels like I'm going to explode with the emotions."

"Hmm." I paused to study the way she took a hold of my dick and held it in place before lowering herself on it inch by inch. "I have plenty of room in mine," I told her, gritting my teeth as pleasure began to shoot through my nerves. "When you feel like you can't contain it, unleash it all on me, sweetheart. I've got you."

And it was true. Truer than it had ever been before. I was the massive brick wall now and Wynnie, the storm that would never stop crashing against it. Her wildness had a home in me forever. She didn't have to be afraid of breaking me anymore and for that, I was always going to be grateful to her. For giving me strength. For making me into this man who had learned not only to fight for himself but for the woman he loves as well.

"I feel like this gives the phrase 'ride or die' a very...literal...meaning," my girlfriend huffed as she worked on me and it made me laugh before I raised myself to sit upright and anchor her body with my own as we carried ourselves towards that place of blissful oblivion.

I was all for building that empire but this right here, having her in my arms, was what truly made me rich. Rich beyond my wildest imagination.

Other Books by STORM

<u>FORBIDDEN series books</u>
<u>'Forbidden' (Book 0.5 - prequel. Jasmine's story.)</u>[1]
<u>'Three's A Crowd' (Book 1)</u>[2]
<u>'Once A Cheater' (Book 2)</u>[3]
<u>'Twice Inflamed' (Book 3)</u>[4]
<u>'Taming Wells' (Book 3.5 - A Jasper Wells novella)</u>[5]
<u>'Shameless' (Book 4)</u>[6]
<u>'Wicked' (Book 5)</u>[7]

And many more...

---

1.   https://www.goodreads.com/book/show/55881993-forbidden

2.   https://www.goodreads.com/book/show/55716260-three-s-a-crowd

3.   https://www.goodreads.com/book/show/55759085-once-a-cheater

4.   https://www.goodreads.com/book/show/55759148-twice-inflamed

5.   https://www.goodreads.com/book/show/55881985-taming-wells

6.   https://www.goodreads.com/book/show/55882058-shameless

7.   https://www.goodreads.com/book/show/55882064-wicked

Aknowledgements

Thank you to each and every 'Girl Obsessed' fan who wanted more Wynnie and Jude content. You made this happen.

About the Author

Come find out at my favourite online hang-out spot. Instagram.

@datcrazywriter_ (Zayn)

Don't miss out!

Visit the website below and you can sign up to receive emails whenever Z. S. STORM publishes a new book. There's no charge and no obligation.

https://books2read.com/r/B-A-TGXR-LFOTC

BOOKS 2 READ

Connecting independent readers to independent writers.

www.ingramcontent.com/pod-product-compliance
Lightning Source LLC
Chambersburg PA
CBHW051252160726
47994CB00003B/1130